WAITING FOR SNOW

words by
MARSHA DIANE ARNOLD

drawings by
RENATA LIWSKA

HOUGHTON MIFFLIN HARCOURT
Boston   New York

For Kate O'Sullivan and Renata Liwska,
a dream editor and illustrator worth waiting for. —M.D.A.

To all those who have patiently waited for me, thank you. —R.L.

The text of this book is set in Janda Safe and Sound.
The illustrations are drawn with pencil and colored digitally.

Library of Congress Catalog Control Number 2015032160
ISBN: 978-0-544-41687-1

Manufactured in Malaysia
TWP 10 9 8 7 6 5 4 3 2 1
4500602458

Hedgehog found Badger staring at the sky.
"What are you doing, Badger?"

"Waiting for snow. It's winter and
I haven't seen one snowflake."

"It will snow in snow's time," said Hedgehog.
"All we have to do is wait."

"I'm tired of waiting," said Badger. He dragged pots and pans and spoons from his house.

"Wake up, Sky! It's time to snow."

Rabbit, Vole, and Possum came flying.
Snow didn't.

"What are you doing, Badger?" asked Rabbit.
"He's trying to make it snow," explained Hedgehog.

"Let's throw pebbles at the sky," said Rabbit. "The pebbles will punch holes in the clouds so the snow can fall through."

Pebbles rained down.
Snow didn't.

"It will never snow," groaned Badger.
"When it's spring, crocus bulbs always bloom," said
Hedgehog, ". . . though sometimes they are late."

"My granny says a snow dance will bring snow," said Vole.
"But it has to be a special dance, danced with good friends."

They stomped and rocked.

They bopped and boogied.

They whirled and swirled.

"It *was* a special dance!" grumped Badger.
"But it didn't bring snow!"

"The sun comes back every day," said Hedgehog,
"and the stars every night."

"I know one more thing to try," said Possum. "Tonight, wear your pajamas backwards. In the morning, we'll have snow. This always works for Possums."

That night Badger put on his pajamas backwards.

In the morning, he hurried outside.
"Snow!" Badger cheered.

"Sugar!" Badger frowned.

"It wasn't snowing this morning," said Hedgehog,
"so we made our own."
Badger plopped on his porch step and moaned.
"Sugar is not snow."

"Crocuses always bloom in spring, the sun rises every morning, stars shine every night," said Hedgehog.

"Sometimes they come late and sometimes early,
but they always come, in their time."

The friends sat beside Badger . . .

and waited . . .

and waited . . .

and waited . . .

appy to see
you

until . . .

it was time.